WELL ROCKED

CLARA BAYARD

ISBN-13: 978-1491252840
ISBN-10: 1491252847

To music, the language of love and pain.

ONE

I stood in the line, wiping at my eyes and trying to pretend I was invisible. Even in the mad crush of people, some were staring at me. It could have been the red-faced weeping. Or the trembling. Whatever it was that caught their attention, the looks of pity were excruciating.

I was feeling a strange combination of agony and numbness. Like my heart was broken, but it hurt too much to actually feel it. It was all too terrible to be real, but I couldn't even soothe myself with thoughts that it was a nightmare. That I hadn't lost everything that mattered in a moment of stupidity.

Before, when Dex and I were alone in that room, he sang to me and I felt like the world was full of possibilities. That I could be anything, do anything. The connection between us was strong and growing every minute. I was reveling in the wildness he brought out in me. I thought our reckless behavior was sexy, a sign of how much we meant to each other.

Now, nose running and eyes starting to swell shut from

crying, I'd never been so humiliated or felt so stupid. And the worst part was I had no one but myself to blame.

From the first second I saw Dex I knew who he was. Every broken man-child I'd seen coming through my father's life and studio growing up. Beautiful and enchanting. But deadly to the hearts of girls like me. Regular girls who could be drawn in, seduced by a spark of something special. He'd dragged me closer physically and emotionally until I was bared completely, defenseless, and giddy with the romance of it all. And then, the first time it mattered, the moment I needed him – he was gone.

I'd supported him, defended him, and helped him deal with his father's illness and what had I gotten in return? Beautiful, empty words to a song.

The sight of my boss, Ryan catching us kissing flashed behind my eyes every time I closed them to shut out the world. He'd warned me, too. That Dex wouldn't be on my side. That he wasn't worth risking a job I loved. A future in the music business that was in my blood.

But did I listen? No. I knew better. No one else was with us when we were alone. No one understood the bond between us. How I understood Dex. How he cared for me.

What a joke. In the back of my mind I'd considered what might happen if we were found out. I imagined some dramatic confrontation. Dex and Ryan nose-to-nose. My boss seething, but resigned. And my lover – my first, my only lover – ferocious and protective.

But instead he'd slunk away and went back to the rest of the band. Back to the people he really cared about. And I was left alone.

"Miss, can I help you?"

I shook my head to clear it a little and looked up at the woman speaking to me. "What?"

"What can I do for you?"

"I-I need a new plane ticket. To America."

She peered at me over wire-rimmed glasses for a long moment and then nodded. "There are not many options, I'm afraid. We have a number of cancellations and delays."

"Yeah, I know. The storm. I'll take whatever you've got. The first thing. I don't care where it lands."

"All right. May I have your ticket, please?"

I shoved it at her and sighed. As my head dipped my hair fell in my face. With a snarl of anger I yanked at it. Gathering the long blond locks at the nape of my neck, I twisted it hard into a bun. It was a motion that usually calmed me, but now it just infuriated. I'd let my hair down, literally and figuratively and now I was ruined. Going back to the States alone with nothing but shattered dreams. And, I realized, nowhere to live. My apartment in Los Angeles had been sublet and my stuff was all in storage. So much for this great adventure.

"Miss, I am very sorry, but I don't think I can book you on anything until tomorrow."

I fought back the urge to snap at her. She was just doing her job, trying to help me. "Oh. Well, okay."

"If it helps, there are reports of tornado sightings nearby. I don't think any flights are leaving the country anytime soon." Rain beat against the windows, hiding the darkening sky from view.

"That's all right. Thanks for trying."

"Of course. Give me one moment to print out your new ticket."

"Thank you." The manners were automatic. Thankful was the last thing I felt. I needed to be in the air. Heading far away from Glasgow, Dex, and everything. But instead I'd be stuck in the airport with hundreds of other people trying

3

to get away. I wondered if any of them were as miserable as me.

After getting my new ticket I trudged away from the desk, elbowing my way through crowds. What had recently been angry stranded travelers had taken a turn. People seemed to have accepted their fate and decided to make the best of it. I passed by groups sitting everywhere, drinking, eating, chatting, having a good time. I hated them all.

Finally I managed to find a relatively quiet spot in a corner. I was debating whether or not to collapse in a heap on the floor when I noticed the crowd parting, and a buzz of excitement running through the open space.

"Please, no," I whispered to myself. "Let this be anyone else."

It was possible. There could be a movie star or some famous athlete in the airport too. The fuss didn't have to be for one of the members of Dream Defiled. The band I'd come to Europe to tour with. The job I'd left my whole life behind for, pointlessly.

But, of course, this was my life and my luck. And with a blotchy, red face and miserable expression full of dread, my gaze locked onto his.

Dex Winters, the band's bassist, was striding over to me. And as much as I loathed him, I couldn't deny how gorgeous he was. Tall and broad-shouldered with chiseled features and over-long, messy black hair, he was sex on legs, and I was speaking from experience. His mouth was set in a hard line, but I remembered the way his lips curled, the way they parted to kiss me everywhere.

I stood up straight and held out a hand to stop him from getting too close. "Don't."

"Where the fuck have you been? Do you have the slightest idea how bloody long I've been looking for you?"

The anger in his voice heightened his British accent, something I'd once found charming and funny. "Liss is weeping, Joe will have probably bribed every guard in this building by now. I can't believe you've run off like that."

"Fuck off, Dex."

He gaped at me for a second, and it seemed everyone in the vicinity shared his surprise. Which made sense. It wasn't often a snotty, red-faced chubby girl told a notoriously sexy rock star to fuck off.

But while I was still reeling from the fact I'd said it out loud, Dex laughed. A full-throated, belly-shaking fit of hilarity. The bastard actually put his hand on my shoulder to steady himself as he tried – and failed – to contain his laughter.

I slapped at the hand and glared at him. "What are you doing?"

He gasped a few times and bent over, hands on his knees. "Christ, woman. You're full of surprises. Here I come to save the day and you're telling me off? Fucking brilliant."

My head was throbbing and I was not in the mood. "What in the world are you talking about? Why are you even here?"

Dex straightened up and looked down at me, his face settling into a serious expression. "I'm here because I don't trust this prat to do what he agreed to."

"Huh?"

He turned around and waved someone over. I was too short to see over his shoulder, so I looked under his arm, and groaned.

"Dex, please. Ryan is the last person – second to last person – I want to see right now."

"Trust me, love, you want to hear what he has to say this time."

5

My former boss stomped over, frowning.

"What's going on?" I asked.

Ryan's frown deepened before he spoke. "Ask your boyfriend here."

I looked over at Dex, who was smiling. "Someone just tell me what the hell is happening so I can get away from you people once and for all. I swear-"

"Becca, wait. Just let Ryan say what he's got to."

The older man shrugged. "This is a mistake."

The smile faded from Dex's face. "Do it. Right now. I won't tell you again."

My eyes widened. I'd never heard him talk to Ryan like that.

"Fine, fine." Ryan cleared his throat. "Rebecca, on further consideration, I believe I may have acted rashly. And I am willing to consider allowing you to continue your work, with a few conditions."

"Huh?" I looked around for someone to make sense of this.

Dex stepped next to me and slung his arm over my shoulder. "He's trying to beg you to come back, in his own pathetic, 'not what we discussed' way."

"Come back? To work? You mean I'm not fired?"

Ryan rolled his eyes. "Well, we'll have to discuss terms, of course. I think a probationary period is very generous, but…yes. I mean you're not fired. Yet."

I looked up at Dex, baffled. "What? How?"

He pulled me tight against his body and squeezed me. "Ryan, why don't you tell her how this happened."

The band's tour manager glowered at both of us. "Dex and the rest of the band threatened to quit. Swore they'd never play another show until I took you back on."

"They what?"

Dex grinned and tilted my chin up so I was looking at him. "Did you think for one second that I would let you go? Let him take you away from me? Because of me?"

A tear slid over my cheek. "I-I guess I did think that."

"You're my girl, Becca. I would never."

A sob bubbled up from my throat but Dex's mouth crashed down on mine, swallowing it. A fresh reserve of tears I'd thought long since shed burst from my eyes as we kissed. My hands fisted in his shirt, holding on for everything. And as applause broke out around us, I was embarrassed and exhilarated and shocked and amazed, but I didn't stop kissing him. To think minutes ago I'd thought I'd never feel that mouth against mine. Never fit the wide spread of my hips against his narrow ones.

"Would you stop that, you're making a scene," Ryan hissed.

Dex barely broke away far enough to reply. "Fuck off."

I giggled, brain completely overloaded. Tucking my head under Dex's chin, I turned to look at Ryan. He was annoyed, but not furious. "Everyone stood up for me?"

From above me, Dex replied. "Well, almost everyone. Rick threw a tantrum and stormed off." He grabbed my arms and pulled me away so we could look each other in the eye. "The rest were there for you. Are here for you."

Swallowing past the lump in my throat, I whispered, "Why?"

"For the smartest girl I know, you're a right idiot sometimes, Becca. They did it because they like you. And respect you. They know how much you've done for all of us. And…because of me. They know I need you."

"I don't know what to say."

"Say yes. Say you'll come back. Stay with me."

I licked my dry lips and nodded. "Yes."

Dex wrapped his arms around me and hugged me so tight I couldn't breathe. He lifted me off my feet for a few seconds and planted a deep, soulful kiss on me. I could hear the click of cameras snapping photos all around us, but I didn't care anymore. Where once I would have been mortified, I was delighted. He'd done it. Showed me that what I felt was real and true. That we were in this together. It was terrifying and wonderful.

TWO

My good mood somehow managed to hold out through the exhaustion caused by the rest of that long day. We spent another six hours at the airport, waiting for storms to clear and backed-up planes to depart. By the time we landed in Paris it was the middle of the night. The band had, of course, missed the charity gig they were supposed to play, which was a shame, but I was secretly glad. Instead of having to be in public, we were able to go right to the hotel when we landed, and I could be alone with Dex.

We rode the elevator with everyone else and I was giddy with the realization that we could go to his room without worrying about being spotted. I didn't plan to throw our relationship in everyone's face, but I wasn't going to hide it anymore. And as long as I did my job, Ryan would let me stay.

Clearly thinking the same thing, Dex kept touching me. A hand on my lower back. Pressing his leg against mine. Lack of sleep and the emotional rollercoaster had left me feeling like I was on drugs, and unsure if I liked it.

But what I knew I definitely liked was walking into Dex's room and shutting the door behind us. Just the two of us, away from the band and the world, if only for a few hours.

As I shoved our bags into a corner, he closed in on me, wrapping his strong arms around my waist.

"This is the strangest fucking day ever."

I giggled. "Pretty much. I'm still a bit in a haze."

He leaned over and nuzzled at my neck. "Need some help winding down, love?"

"Mm. Sounds good." It felt good too, but there was one thing I needed to do first. "But hold that thought. I need to talk to you."

"No, no, no," he murmured against my skin. "No more talking."

"Come on. Give me five minutes."

He licked the line of my jaw, sighed and then pulled back. "Fine. But hurry. I'm knackered but I won't sleep tonight without getting my hands on you."

I smiled and my stomach flipped, but tried to concentrate. Taking a deep breath, I stepped away from him and perched on the edge of a plush chair by the window. "I owe you an apology, Dex."

He sprawled out on the bed on his side, facing me. "No you don't."

"Yes, I do." I looked down at my hands, feeling ashamed of myself. "I didn't trust you. I didn't believe you. Didn't believe in us. That was wrong."

"I understand. You were freaked out. I was freaked out."

"That doesn't excuse what I thought. I was furious with you. Disappointed in you."

10

Dex sat up then, hair falling in his eyes. "Becca, it's fine. I haven't exactly given you a lot of reasons to have faith in me. But that's going to change. When Ryan caught us and fired you, I felt sick. With him, with myself, with everything. You've done so much for me, been there for me. Hell, I wouldn't have had the stones to go see my father, let alone convince Ryan to let me. Not without you right there next to me. Fighting for me. Helping me be strong instead of a coward."

I shook my head as tears filled my eyes. "You're no coward. Honey, you're my hero. I was just so scared, so upset that I forgot it."

He slid off the bed and knelt in front of me, taking my hands in his. "I should have said something, but I was panicking. I know Ryan, how his brain works. I was just focused on making him change it, I didn't think about how you'd be feeling right then. I was trying to fix it, but should have taken a minute to talk to you about what I was planning."

I squeezed his fingers. "How did it happen, anyway?"

He grinned. "As soon as you ran out, he got on the phone. I huddled with everyone and told them what had happened, and what I was going to do. Honestly, I never thought of asking them to join in, but they did. You need to know that. Matthew and Joe were ready. Liss was fuming. Even Steve was willing to quit if Ryan wouldn't hire you back.

We went to him as a group. He tried to brush us off but I wouldn't let him. I looked him in the eye and told him there would be no tour without you. He laughed at first, but when the others agreed, I could see the anger in him turn to fear. He knew we were serious. And knew he'd be out of a job too if he didn't relent. The label and rest of our management doesn't give a shit who I'm kissing, but they sure as hell would care if we cancelled the next two weeks' worth of dates and lost all the money they laid out for this."

It was inspiring and moving to hear the emotion in his voice as he explained. See the intensity in his eyes. "Thank you."

Dex pulled my hands to his chest. "Don't thank me. Just know that you've changed my life. Changed who I am. And there's nothing in the world that I can ever do to repay that. But I'm sure as shit going to try."

I was crying again, but didn't care. I kissed him, sliding off the chair as I wrapped my arms around his neck. We landed in the floor in a heap of tangled limbs, but didn't stop to move into a more comfortable position. Dex's tongue snaked between my lips, tasting me. I dug my fingers into the thick hair hanging over the neck of his t-shirt and pressed my body close against his.

Kissing him was like drowning in beauty. Overwhelming, he took my breath away, but left desire, a desperate need for his touch behind.

His hands dipped under my shirt and I sighed.

"You like that?" he asked against my mouth.

"I like everything you do to me."

"Good."

I held him tighter and we started to roll over, but banged into the side of the bed. "Ouch."

Dex chuckled. "Careful."

I groaned. "As sexy as this is, I think we should get off the floor."

"Why?"

"Because we've been traveling and sitting and standing all day. I was sore when we walked in the door, this isn't helping."

He poked me in the side, smiling. "You sound like an old woman, Becca."

"I feel like one."

"Well then, I have a solution." He took my hand as he stood, pulling me up with him.

"Old-age home?"

"Much better." His eyes twinkled and his lip curled. "Co-ed shower."

"Sounds dangerous."

"Don't worry. I'll hold on to you."

"I bet." I laughed as he tried to drag me to the bathroom and pull off my clothes at the same time. Dex was always so smooth and sexy; I enjoyed him not quite being able to manage a maneuver. Then I stopped and helped him, concerned he might rip something in his haste.

We made it into the bathroom without any damage and both stripped down quickly. The light wasn't on, so the only illumination in the room was what came through the door. It felt romantic and I appreciated not having to look at myself under glaring whiteness.

The shower stall was large and glass-walled, with two showerheads, one on each wall. I twisted them both on full heat and stepped inside. Dex followed quickly, and I had a few seconds to enjoy the long, muscular stretch of his body, the width of his shoulders and what looked like miles of smooth skin.

He arched an eyebrow as he stepped under the spray with me. "Enjoying the view?"

I nodded. "I love looking at you."

"And I love feeling your eyes on me." His hand reached around to tug my hair free and then spread it over my shoulders where it darkened under the water.

"You spend all your life with eyes on you."

13

"Not yours."

"Are they different?"

"Better."

I grinned and hugged him as steam surrounded us and the pounding of the water drowned out everything. A private oasis for two. Peaceful and soothing. But when my body pressed against his, I felt Dex's arousal, long and thick between us, and peace was the last thing I wanted.

Feeling a wave of sex-fueled energy come over me, I grabbed the soap and lathered up my hands before running them down his chest. Dex's eyes fluttered as my fingers slid over his pecs and flat nipples, down the ridges of his abs, and lower.

He scooped up some of the suds and returned the favor, slipping his hands over my shoulders and down my back. It was, strangely, more intimate than when we'd actually slept together. Even though I could barely see him in the steam and dark room, I felt bared to him in a new way. One that made me nervous, but I liked it.

When my hands encountered his slip hips, his lower body jerked, sending his erection against my palms. Shifting us so the spray could wash away the soap, I decided shower time was about to be over. Getting clean was now very low on my list of priorities.

I started pulling his face down to mine, gripping his shoulder with one hand while the other circled the base of his cock.

"That is even better than your eyes," he said, voice husky.

"What?"

"Your hands. Your tiny little hands."

I laughed. "They're not tiny."

"Yes, they are."

"Shut up."

"Kiss me again and I'll never say another word about your wee little hands."

I rolled my eyes and bit back a giggle, and then kissed him. It was soft at first, then harder. Our tongues tangled and twisted and teeth scraped. It was messy and hurried. Hungry.

"Christ, Becca," he said, breathlessly after a long moment. "I need to have you. Right now."

I buried my face against his chest, feeling it rise and fall as my fingers slid over his thickening flesh. "Not in here."

"Why not?"

Looking up, I shoved down my desire in order to answer him. "We could slip. Or get burned. Or the shower might leak. Plus we don't-"

Dex pressed a finger over my lips to stop me. "I get it," he said sharply, but the look of affection on his face softened it. "Skip the list-making and come to bed."

I just nodded. We turned off the water and, holding hands, made our way, dripping, across the tiled floor back to the bedroom.

Within a flash we were on the bed, arms back around each other, lips pressed together. I shivered a bit in the cool air on my wet skin, and Dex yanked at the blanket at the bottom of the bed, pulling it over us.

I smiled and tucked my body against his. "This is much better. And more comfortable."

"True. Does that mean you just want to cuddle?"

"Not a chance."

"Thank fuck for that, love. I need to be inside you."

My heart thundered in my chest and my core clenched at his words. "Yes, please."

Dex chuckled, and then kissed me on the neck, sliding

slowly down my body as he rolled me over onto my back. When his face was even with my breasts he kissed the puckered tips of each one before drawing circles with his tongue on one and the tips of his on the other. He did that for a few moments and then switched sides, letting me feel the difference in pressure, moisture and intensity. My whole body quivered and my hips flexed, thighs spreading unconsciously, bidding him closer to where I wanted him – needed him – most.

He shifted positions, but didn't stop. His waist rested in the cradle of my legs, and he reached down to stroke the wide expanse of my hip. "Shit, I love your body. So lush and full. Soft and responsive."

That wasn't exactly how I saw it, but I could appreciate his words. And couldn't argue with the last part. Every bit of me responded to his touch. A finger on my lips sent sparks of pleasure down to my toes. A stroke on my skin went through to my bones.

"I can feel you disagreeing. Stop it. See yourself the way I see you. Feel how perfect and sexy you are."

I started to speak, but his teeth circled my nipple and bit down gently. The only sound I made was a low moan.

"That's my girl." Dex released my breast and slid down further. His face lowered against my body, hair ticking at my belly. He used two fingers to spread me open, baring my moist heat to the air, and then covered me with his mouth.

My fingers fisted in the sheets and I bit down on my lower lip. "Dex…"

He didn't speak, only flicked his tongue over the tiny bundle of nerves over my folds, and slid one thick finger inside me.

I groaned and tossed my head, back arching.

Dex made a pleased sound low in his throat and kept

16

up the sweet, erotic torture, coaxing pleasure from my body easily, as if he knew every spot and speed and amount of pressure to drive me wild.

And as a quick, sharp climax ripped through me, wild is exactly what I was. A hoarse, strangled sound burst from my mouth and my body started undulating in time with the waves of ecstasy rolling through me.

It was as if every bit of tension and fear left hiding within me exploded out, pushed away by pleasure. I felt lighter down to my soul and couldn't do anything but go with it, let it take me away.

But Dex wouldn't let me depart the moment completely. His movement slowed, but didn't cease. He touched me just enough to keep me grounded, aware that he was with me, taking me on this journey. There weren't words to express how I felt, and he didn't need them. My body, open and honest in a way I wasn't capable of being, said everything. He rode out the orgasm with me, and when my eyes opened and looked down, his gaze was locked on my face, a look of wonder and pride across his.

I made a contented sound and had to clear my throat before I could speak. "Sorry, I got a little carried away there."

He smiled. "It was wonderful."

"Not for you."

"Oh yes it was. Watching you come is amazing. But I am not entirely selfless. Nor am I anywhere close to being done with you tonight."

"Really? Because I am kind of sleepy now."

Dex grunted and reared up before coming down on top of me again, this time with his face next to mine. He nipped at my neck and lifted my legs up around his waist. "Not even close to done, Becca."

I could feel the thick heat of him against my body and

17

I smiled. "Maybe not too sleepy."

"Good." His hips rolled and he pressed against my damp folds. "Please tell me you can reach my trousers without leaving this bed."

I reached out an arm. "Barely."

"Good thing, because I need something in there and I don't think I'm capable of letting you go right now."

With a nod I grabbed the pants he'd shed, and reached into the pocket. I handed the foil packet over to him and in seconds he'd spread the condom over his length and was back in position, nudging the entrance of my sex with the blunt tip of his member.

"Sure you're not too tired?"

I hissed and lifted my hips in response.

Dex chuckled and then pushed inside me, invading and filling slowly, but relentlessly.

Like the first time, it was a snug and deliciously aching fit. My body was as ready as possible, but Dex was a big boy all over. Taking him inside me was like being taken over by him. Consumed, I existed only as sensation, wild and beautiful. The feeling was addictive and I was happily hooked.

Dex brushed a lock of hair from my face and lowered his so we were close enough to kiss. But instead, he stayed there, breath puffing against my lips as our lower bodies moved in that ancient rhythm.

I lifted my head to kiss him, but he pulled back, whispering, "I just want to watch you."

That was new and crazy and wonderful, too.

I nodded and wrapped my arms around him, sliding my hands down the length of his back, feeling his muscles clench and release as I went.

My touch seemed to inflame him, and Dex started

driving into me deeper and harder, panting as he moved, but still watching my face with total attention. The scrutiny started to embarrass me a little. I wondered briefly if I was making a weird expression or if my wet hair looked stupid.

But then, as if he could tell I was drifting, Dex slipped a finger between us and rubbed at my clit while he drove in and out of me, banishing any semblance of thought from my head, filling the space with us. The feel of his skin against mine, the scent of soap and water. The soft sounds of our coupling, the heat stoking hotter and hotter deep within me.

It was all too much and I couldn't take it and never wanted it to stop. I cried out as he shifted his hips to a new angle, and he gritted his teeth and then let go, flying off the cliff with me into an ocean of pleasure where we floated forever.

THREE

The next morning I woke up groggy and grumpy, until I noticed the long arm slung across my body and remembered where I was.

Dex mumbled something unintelligible and pulled me closer.

"Good morning," I said, sinking happily into his embrace.

"The only thing that's ever good about morning is when you're the first thing I see."

I smiled and closed my eyes, wondering how I could possibly be this lucky. With all the shit I'd seen and gone through, I'd somehow ended up in Paris, waking up in the arms of a sexy, talented man. At first I thought there were no words for what I was feeling, but then it became clear there was one. Love.

I couldn't count how many songs I knew about falling in love, but it occurred to me that they were all right, and all wrong. I was falling for Dex, hard. And it was impossible that anyone had ever felt this way. The voice of caution in my head was silent for the first time in as long as I could remember, and I was glad. Nothing would ruin this moment. Whatever happened in the future, we would always have this morning, this perfect time where we were alone together with nothing to do but be with each other, no doubts or obligations to get in the way.

Rolling over to face Dex, I smiled. He was beautiful as always, dark eye bright and chiseled features stubbled, but his hair was a disaster. It had dried in bed and was matted in some places and sticking up in other.

"What's so funny?"

"Nothing," I replied, unconvincing.

"Liar."

"Your hair is terrible. But you're still perfect."

He snarled playfully and planted a light kiss on my lips.

I sighed and snuggled in closer, wondering if he was feeling even the slightest bit as happy as I was. "What are you thinking about?"

"Two things."

"And they are?"

"Eating breakfast and making you scream again."

I laughed. "Are you deciding between them?"

"Not exactly. More like figuring out how to combine them. I'm a greedy man. I want both."

"Hm. Good luck with that. But if I get a vote, I say we go for breakfast."

"A vote? You get anything you want." He kissed me again, deeper this time, with purpose.

"Behave, Dex."

"Never."

"Good." I smiled and reluctantly dragged myself away from him. Wrapping the sheet around me I hopped off the bed.

"Where are you going?"

"To finish that shower."

"I'll join you."

I glanced at him over my shoulder. "No, you won't."

He stuck out his lower lip, pouting.

"Cute. But that won't work on me."

Dex grinned. "What am I supposed to do all by myself?"

"Order us some breakfast."

That inspired him. He jumped up and went over to the table where the room service menu sat and grabbed it. I took a long moment to stare at his naked body. He was so unselfconscious about walking around naked. I envied that. But, if I was that perfect I'd probably do the same.

With a sigh of regret I went into the bathroom and shut the door behind me.

When I finished in there and went back to the bedroom, Dex was still naked, sitting at the foot of the bed, watching television.

I tugged my towel tighter around me and walked over to join him. "Is the food coming? One of us should be dressed enough to open the door."

He didn't say anything, so I looked up at the screen to see what had entranced him. It was a news report in French, so I couldn't understand more than a word here and there. The reporter was standing in front of a large map of Europe. I was about to ask why he was watching the weather so closely when the map disappeared and crappy cell-phone video of a very familiar scene started to play.

It was from the airport. On the screen Dex was walking towards the camera and I could see Ryan's face at the edge of the frame, behind him. There was audio, but you couldn't hear what Dex said over the background noise from the crowded waiting area.

Form the angle, the person with the camera had been standing near me, so I never appeared on screen. But watching the scene play out, it was like being back there.

"What is this?"

Dex finally snapped out of it. "Us."

"I can see that. But why is it on TV?"

He shrugged. "I have no idea. I don't speak French."

"There are channels in English here, silly."

"Yeah, of course. Didn't think of that."

I took the remote from him and flipped through the channels. Finally I heard English and stopped. They weren't showing the same video, but I saw still photos from the airport. These were from earlier, before everything got crazy.

There was Dex again, this time standing next to Matthew, laughing about something. Off to his right I could see myself, facing away from the camera, talking to one of the airline employees. My butt looked about twenty miles wide, but I didn't have time to be annoyed, as the announcer's voice began speaking again.

"Historic storms blanketed the country, stranding thousands of people and delaying hundreds of flights. Reports throughout Western Europe indicate there are still travelers struggling to make it to their destinations, though things are close to getting back to normal in the past few hours. So, while international rock sensations Dream Defiled may have made it where they were going after a drama-filled day, many others were not so lucky. Two of the tornados spotted yesterday have been confirmed as being responsible for the devastation outside Glasgow. Our James Carren is reporting life from the scene."

"Holy shit," I muttered.

"Crazy."

23

"Well, this should make Ryan happy. If every story about the storms mentions you guys, he'll be in heaven."

Dex nodded and bumped my shoulder with his. "I guess we were a bit busy with our shit to notice what was really going on."

"Yeah, I guess we were." I was thinking about that when there was a knock on the door.

"Food, finally," Dex said, rising.

I grabbed my suitcase and dragged it towards the bathroom. "Put some pants on before you open that, please."

"Getting possessive already, Becca? I like it." He winked at me and strolled over to the door, still naked.

Rolling my eyes, I went back into the bathroom to get dressed in private.

A few hours later we were fed and dressed, and I'd practically forgotten about the news reports. After checking in with Ryan I was shocked to discover he didn't have anything for me to do until later, so Dex and I actually had time to do whatever we wanted. We had a serious discussion about staying in, that mainly consisted of him grabbing me and dragging me down onto the bed, but I finally managed to convince him we should spend at least a little bit of time in Paris actually out in Paris.

We were standing in front of the hotel, surrounded by lush plants and fragrant flowers, trying to decide what to do first.

"What about the *Louvre*? I think the tourist trap tower can wait until it's dark, so we can see it all lit up, go up and watch the city."

"Okay. Or we can just wander. See what we find."

"Uh-huh." I looked down at my phone; scrolling through the app I'd downloaded. "There are five great museums within walking distance. Or we could grab a cab across the river and visit *Père Lachaise*. I know you want to see Jim Morrison's grave." I paused. "Yeah, we should do that. I can map a route over in that section of the city, make sure we're not wasting time backtracking or…" I trailed off at the sound of laughter. "What?"

Dex was grinning broadly. "Using a map and a plan really is your idea of wandering, isn't it?"

I blushed and shoved my phone back in my purse. "Kind of. I know, I know. I'm so boring."

"Not in the slightest. Just organized." He slung an arm over my shoulder and we started walking toward the sidewalk. "Try it my way today, okay? We'll just walk and see what we see?"

"Okay, sure. That sounds fun."

"You mean it sounds terrible, I can tell. But you'll like it, I promise."

I thought about all the things Dex and I had done. All the rules I'd broken to be with him. This was minor, and so far he'd been right. I'd been having the time of my life. So if he wanted to wander, I would wander. "All right. No plan, no map. Just fun."

"That's my girl," he said, leaning over to kiss me on the top of my head.

I smiled and wrapped an arm around his waist. As long as we were together, I really didn't care where were went or what we did. It would be wonderful.

And it was. For a while. We strolled around; down streets I'd heard of and seen in movies and many I couldn't even pronounce. Past amazing smells emanating from little shops, and groups of loud tourists. We stopped at a little flower stand and Dex got me a single, perfect rose. He snapped off the bloom and tucked it behind my ear after releasing my hair from its bun.

I laughed at the cheese gesture, but secretly loved it. I was starring in my own romantic film and couldn't stop smiling.

Eventually we both needed a rest, so we found a little café and went inside. It was quintessential Paris, to me. Tiny tables full of lazy diners sipping drinks and nibbling at tiny pastries. We grabbed the last table outside, half under the awning, and sighed in unison.

I laughed. "Wandering is tiring."

"So it seems. I could really use a pint right now."

"I doubt they serve beer here. Wine, maybe."

Dex shrugged. "Doesn't matter. We can drink later."

Silently, I thanked him for saying that. I wanted a clear head for this whole wonderful experience and was glad to see he – at least for the moment – felt the same way.

After poring over the menu we ordered coffees and a selection of…something. It cost a lot, so I was hoping for the best.

Dex was leaning back in his seat with sunglasses shielding his eyes from the sun. He'd thoughtfully given me the chair in the shade. I loved seeing him like that. Relaxed and content, but totally present. Since we first met most of the time he was happy, there was a bottle in his hand. I had worried that the stress of his father's illness and our visit there, coupled with the drama with me and Ryan would still be bothering him, but he seemed genuinely blissful and at peace.

Of course, that only lasted a little while. By the time our

drinks arrived I'd noticed a group of people down the street staring at us. Four girls a little younger than me and three guys around the same age, they were all dressed in trendy styles that looked just this side of sloppy. It was a look I'd seen a lot, and I knew it cost a lot of money to accomplish.

After thanking the waiter, I leaned over to ask Dex about them. "See those people down there? They're looking over here. Do you know them?"

He turned his head and lifted his sunglasses to look. "Nope. Never seen them before."

"Hm." I glanced over again and now they were huddled together, having what looked like a spirited debate.

"Don't worry, love. They probably just think you're beautiful."

"Yeah, right." I rolled my eyes and took a sip of my iced coffee. It was rich and delicious. "I hope they're not autograph hounds or something."

"I doubt that." He shoved the glasses into his pocket and leaned over to take my hand. "You're not on duty today. Just have fun."

"I know. I just…"

"Can't help it. I noticed." He flashed a dazzling grin that had me forgetting all about the people looking at us.

Just then the waiter brought over our food. It was a tower of stunning desserts, a dozen different bite-size pieces of heaven. "Oh, wow," was all I managed.

Dex chuckled, but I could see his hand creeping close to the plate, itching to try something.

Our eyes met and we both dug in. At first we aimed for nonchalant and civilized, but as each sweet confection exploded my taste buds, I soon found myself cramming them in as fast as I could chew.

With his mouth full, Dex grinned at me.

"Gross, honey," I said."

"Sorry. But I needed to tell you this before I slip into a sugar coma."

"What?" I popped a tiny tart with a raspberry on top into my mouth.

"We're coming here for every meal, agreed?" He crunched down on a flaky pastry dripping with honey.

"Deal."

In the middle of a dark chocolate something-or-other, I happened to look up and see that the randoms looking at us had moved. Now they were a few feet away, jostling each other, staring at us again.

One of them broke off from the pack and walked closer, standing on the opposite side of the table next to us. The older couple sitting at the table glared at the girl, but she seemed oblivious. I was sure what she'd say even before she opened her mouth.

"Are you Dex Winters?" she asked in an American accent.

I sighed as Dex swallowed down whatever he was eating, and plastered on a smile.

"I sure am."

"Oh my god. I *knew* it! How crazy is this, seeing you here. What are you doing?"

He glanced over at me. "Just hanging. What's your name?"

"Jasmine. Um…look. I know this is really uncool, but would you take a picture with me and my friends? We're huge fans."

Dex stood up. "Of course. I'd be happy to. But let's move down a bit, yeah? Let these nice people enjoy their afternoon."

She nodded so vigorously I thought she might strain

something. "Yeah, okay. Of course. Whatever you say."

While he ushered her away from the table, past all of the annoyed Parisians, I flagged down our waiter to get the check. Obviously the normal couple hanging out portion of the day was over.

By the time I'd paid and followed Dex, he was in the middle of a rather elaborate photo shoot with the group. Each one wanted a picture alone with him, then one with some of their friends, then the rest.

Eventually they ran out of configurations, until they spotted me. Half a dozen phones were shoved into my hands and they gathered in a clump for a group picture. I idly wondered where Mia was. This kind of thing would have been her job. But then I remembered she was the one who outed me and Dex to Ryan, and decided not to think about her at all anymore.

I snapped a series of pictures and handed the phones back to their respective owners, only half listening to the conversation Dex was having with them. It was bitchy of me to be irritated, but I couldn't help it. Fans or not, they were invading my time with Dex, and I hated that. Plus I knew he'd never be rude to them and we might end up standing on the sidewalk all day.

A tall, skinny guy with sandy hair was asking Dex questions so fast I could barely understand him. "We saw on the news that you guys were in Paris, but we never thought we'd actually see you. Is the rest of the band here?"

"No, just me and Becca."

"Oh, cool. Do you know where the other guys are? Don't you all chill together all the time?"

Dex chuckled. "We spend plenty of time together. I assume they're off seeing the city or sleeping off last night, depending on the man."

"Ha, yeah, I bet. You guys sure know how to party. Say, we're heading over to this bar we found yesterday. Do you wanna come along?"

My eyes widened. "Isn't it a little early for bars?"

The guy laughed. "Not here. They drink all day. It's cool. Plus we can all get served."

"Well that's something to celebrate for sure," Dex said. "Why not."

I glared at him briefly. "Dex, can I talk to you alone for a second?"

He nodded and came over to me. But before I could remind him that we were supposed to be spending the day together, and that I'd be working and with Liss the next day, I saw the rest of the group hear the news that Dex was going to hang out with them. Excitement was an understatement. I thought a few of them would overcome gravity they bounced so hard with happiness.

With a sigh I looked at Dex. "Never mind."

He held my chin in one hand. "It'll just be a few drinks, love. They told me they tried to get tickets to the show but couldn't. An hour of my time is the least I can do for them."

"I know."

"Hey, I know this isn't the romantic day you wanted. But we've got all night, right?"

"Of course."

"You're not cross?"

I shook my head. And it was true. I was disappointed more than anything. And annoyed with myself for being so selfish. Without the fans there would have been no European tour and no job for me. I owed them just as much as the band did.

That thought struck me hard, and I made a decision. "Look, why don't you go with them. Have fun. I'll go back to the hotel and get a little work done. That way we can have more time together later."

"You sure? I want you to come along."

"Nah, it's fine. Be your charming self. I'll be waiting for you."

"If you promise to be waiting naked I'll tell these guys to bugger off in five minutes."

I laughed and slapped his arm. "Go be a rock star."

FOUR

It was close to midnight before I saw Dex again, back at the hotel. He'd sent a text a few hours earlier, so I knew he was fine, just having too much fun and too many drinks to leave. Instead of having dinner with me and going to see the Eiffel Tower, he went on whatever the French version of a bar crawl is with a bunch of strangers.

Sitting in my room alone, I'd sworn I wouldn't yell at him. After all, his unpredictable nature and love of partying was part of what I liked about him, right? Hadn't I just been relishing the way he dragged out of my comfort zone?

As the hours wore on I couldn't figure out if I was being unreasonable or not. To me it seemed rude and dismissive for him to bail like that. But I had told him to go have fun. And if I really wanted to spend time with him I could have called and asked him to come back, or offered to meet him somewhere. Hating the lack of clarity, I just stewed for a while. I only left my room to go down to the restaurant for a quick dinner. It was full of gorgeous couples mocking me with their happiness. What the hell was up with Paris, anyway, I wondered. Did they only allow beautiful people to move into the city and breed?

In full grump mode, I went back upstairs. I spent a little time working – returning emails and checking logistics for the Paris shows and travel arrangements for the rest of the tour. Normally, going down my list, rechecking and confirming would make me feel better. This time it just annoyed me more.

So, by the time Dex knocked on my door, I was a mass of irritation. I let him in and was immediately enveloped in a tight hug. He stank like cigarettes and booze, reminding me of my father.

When I was little he'd get home late and always come in to kiss me goodnight. Sometimes it soothed me, the scent of his lifestyle wafting through the air when he opened my bedroom door, lingering on my pillow when he bent to kiss my forehead. But as I got older than smell came to represent everything I was missing. My dad was a visitor in my life at best, even though I lived with him.

And now, after hours of waiting for Dex, I couldn't get that thought out of my mind, that I was falling for a man just like my father. Was this my future with him? Sitting at home, waiting for him to come back and kiss me goodnight?

"God, I've missed you," he said into my hair.

I pulled out of the hug and went back to sit on the bed. "How was your night?"

"Lovely. Don't let the fancy fool you. This city is full of real drinkers." He sauntered over and threw himself down on the bed next to me, stretching out. "Are we sleeping in here tonight?"

I answered through gritted teeth. "I am."

"Where you go, I go, love."

It took every ounce of control I had not to scoff at

33

that, considering how we'd spent our respective evenings.

"Look, I'm tired. I just want to get some rest. I've got a lot to do tomorrow before I go shopping with Liss."

He shrugged and rolled over to face me. "That's all right. But if you just want to sleep, do you mind if I go out for a while? I'm a bit restless tonight."

"Sure, fine. I guess I'll see you in the morning."

Dex sat up. He looked at me for a while with his head cocked to the side. "Yeah, okay. How about a goodnight kiss?"

"Of course." I was annoyed with him, but that didn't keep me from wanting him. As our lips met I considered changing my mind. Convincing him to stay with me in bed, make him forget about partying or anything except how hot we were together.

But as the taste of liquor transferred from his mouth to mine, it smothered the rising heat inside me. I broke off the kiss and said goodbye.

Dex got up and headed for the door. He turned back. "You okay, love?"

"Yes. Just tired."

His eyes narrowed for a moment, but then he shrugged again and turned away.

I sat on the bed by myself for a long time after the door slammed behind him, wondering how one day could change how I felt so much.

The next afternoon I was at another café. This one was noticeably less fancy than the one I'd visited with Dex, but I didn't mind. Liss and I were sitting outside the tiny place that I imagined was quite a popular dive bar at night. She was having a glass of red wine to steady her nerves, and I was sipping a coffee.

"How wild is this, Becca?"

I smiled. "What, the two of us having a drink a block away from the *Moulin Rouge*, or you getting ready to get your first tattoo?"

Her face paled. "Both, I guess. I'm trying not to think about the torture. I mean – the tattoo."

I laughed. "It really isn't that bad. It doesn't feel good or anything, but it's survivable."

"Well I hope so. Joe would be pretty pissed if I died getting some ink without even telling him."

"Why are you keeping it a secret? Planning to get his name across your ass?"

She sputtered, choking on a sip of wine. "No. To be honest, I wasn't going to tell anyone, in case I chickened out. But when I called they told me I had to have a consultation first, which made me feel better. And then after I checked it out yesterday, I was feeling a bit braver. But I still might run away. I figured you wouldn't tell on me."

"Of course not. Though, if I were you I'd be more worried about getting inked up at a place named after a cartoon character."

She grinned. "That is not helping. But seriously, were you scared when you got yours?"

I rubbed my shoulder over the t-shirt that covered my ink. "Not really. Everyone I knew growing up had lots of them, though. Even the wusses. So I figured I could take it."

Liss giggled. "I clearly brought the right person. If Joe was with me I don't know what he'd do. Either tease me mercilessly or punch the guy if I looked like I was in pain. Either way, I'm glad he's not here."

"Me too. And even though this isn't exactly the shopping trip I was hoping for, it's great to spend some time away from the boys."

She sighed and slouched down in her seat. "I hear that. Don't tell, but part of the reason I'm on this trip is to get it out of my system. I figured a couple of weeks trapped with the whole gang would leave me dying to start school at the end of next month."

I nodded.

"Shit," she continued. "You almost got fired. Probably not the time to make jokes about getting away from all of this."

"It's okay. It was hard, but at least I don't have to lie anymore about Dex and me."

Something in my voice must have clued her in that things weren't exactly perfect. She leaned over and put her hand over mine. "Are you okay?"

"Sure."

"Come on. Even terrified as I am, I can see something's wrong. Do you want to talk about it?"

"Not really. I mean, yeah, I'd love your opinion. But I'm worried I'll seem like a bitch."

"We haven't known each other very long, but I *know* you're not a bitch. It's something about Dex? Just tell me."

I crossed my arms and looked down at the table. "Yeah."

"Did you have a fight?"

"Not exactly." I went on to explain everything that had happened yesterday. Talking about it made me even more annoyed.

"Uh-huh, that's a tough one," Liss said once I was finished. "Neither one of you really did anything wrong, but I can see why you're upset with him."

"It isn't like I expect him to spend every free second

with me. But...I don't know. I guess it just reminded me that things aren't as perfect as they seemed."

She smiled. "Now that I completely understand. It's easy to get carried away in the fairytale of this. The sexy rocker and the regular girl. But this is real. They're real people, not fictional princes. If you forget that, you're bound to be disappointed, if not crushed."

"Hm, yeah. You're right. And I'm not naïve. I know he cares for me. But there's a darkness in him. Damage I can relate to, but don't really understand. He hides it well, and sometimes I forget."

"Dex is a good guy."

"Of course. I know that. He's amazing. But, I just worry. It's only been a few days since he went to see his dad, and he's pretending it never happened. I know he must be thinking about it, but he doesn't say a word."

"Did you ask him?"

"No. I don't want to push. And there's been enough drama lately."

"Now that is an understatement. Did you see our faces all over the television?"

"Ugh, yes. Don't remind me. I'm just glad no one caught the scene I made."

Liss smiled and finished her glass of wine. "Dex said you really laid into him."

"I did. I was...really upset."

"I can imagine. Hey, speaking of upset. What the hell is up with Mia? Do you know why she narced on you?"

"I have no idea. She always seemed a little distant, but I didn't expect her to do that."

"Me either. I haven't seen her since we got to the hotel, have you?"

"No. Which is a good thing. I don't want to get fired all

over again for going crazy on Ryan's niece."

"Ha. I'd like to see that. I don't know where she gets off anyway. She barely does any work."

"Don't remind me. I've got to find someone else to work on the blog. She hasn't posted anything in days."

"No need, I guess. Every move is getting tons of coverage from the gossip sites."

I groaned. "Even worse. How are you so chill about that?"

She shrugged. "I don't read them. Sometimes my best friend Kelly forwards me stuff she thinks is funny, but otherwise I ignore it. Oh, except for one time. A blog identified me as Joe's cousin and speculated that I was mooching off of him, complete with fake photos of cars and shit he supposedly bought me. Where the hell did they get that idea?"

"Made it up."

"Clearly. It's just wrong."

"I assume that's not the kind of journalism you'll be studying."

"Hell no."

We shared a laugh, and I realized I was starting to feel better. Liss had a calming influence. She seemed so self-assured and secure. In her relationship and herself. And from what the guys had told me, she went from being a waitress to girlfriend of Joe Hawk in no time flat. If she could manage, so could I. I hoped. Not that our situations were the same. Joe was on his way to becoming a super-star, but he was pretty well-adjusted and completely devoted to her.

"Wow, I guess I really did need to talk. Thank you."

She smiled. "No problem. Listen, I don't know what the solution is, really. Dex has some real issues to deal with, things you can't make disappear. But he's great. And worth the trouble, I think. When Joe and I were going through some stuff, Dex was a good friend to both of us. And I see how happy he is around you."

"I feel the same way."

"Good. So just go with the flow, you know? See how things shake out. If the past few weeks have shown us anything, it should be that anything can happen. Life changes so fast. Take what good you can."

I shook my head. "I hear what you're saying. But that is *so* not me. I like to plan things, organize. Know what my options are and the possible repercussions."

"That, my friend, is what makes you good at your job. But love doesn't work that way. Never has, never will."

"I never said anything about love."

She leaned forward and patted my shoulder. "You didn't have to."

I sighed deeply. "That obvious?"

"To me? Yeah. You wouldn't be this freaked out if your feelings weren't so strong."

"But it's so fast. Too fast."

"Does telling yourself that change how you feel?"

"Nope."

"Well, there's your answer, then."

"Fair enough." I frowned, looking down at my watch. "Hey, it's about that time. We should pay and get out of here."

"Oh shit."

"Sorry, relationship guru. Time for you to get tatted up."

"You won't tell anyone if I faint, right?"

"Our secret. No one but me will know what a big baby you are."

39

Liss scrunched her nose at me and then smiled. "Okay, okay. Let's get this over with before I lose my nerve."

We paid the check and walked across the street to the tattoo place. A guy with amazingly intricate sleeve-work was sitting behind the counter and welcomed us. Liss went off for her appointment after casting one last look of fear over her shoulder. I smiled reassuringly and waved, making my way over to the seating area.

While I waited for her, I checked my email and voicemail. Ryan had forwarded a ton of things that I just skimmed, figuring I could dig in later on my computer. But one message caught my eye. Sales figures from the label, which came in often, but there was something else in the email chain. A mention of someone called Julia Connor. The name sounded familiar, but I couldn't place it. I considered looking her up, but got distracted by the rest of the message. Based on what I saw, the new album, *Not Keeping Score*, was already about to go platinum and based on projections might even double. That was huge. The label had taken a real risk on the guys after the first one. It had sold well, but nothing amazing. The new contract had really been won based on the attention the guys were receiving, and the extremely obvious fact that Joe was born to be a super star.

It was great, and my first thought was to tell Dex. But I hesitated, and then was annoyed with myself for it. I needed to follow Liss's advice. Instead of worrying about any of the million possible bad things that might happen, I should enjoy us.

So I called his room at the hotel. It was clear from his voice that he'd just woken up.

"Did you get some rest?"

"Yes. Slept like the dead."

"Hangover?"

"Seven out of ten."

"Poor baby."

"Becca, that was not at all sympathetic. You sound positively gleeful."

I laughed, letting the sexy sound of his sleepy voice soothe away my last doubts. "I am, but not about that."

"What, then?"

"I've got some top secret info."

He chuckled. "Good. Tell me."

"I was just reading my emails and the album is doing incredibly well. Like platinum well."

"No shit?"

"No shit."

"That's great news. I'd hate to have to get a real job."

"No chance of that now. I'm really happy for you."

"Us, love. Be happy for us. You're part of the family now, whether you like it or not."

"I do like it."

"Good. Are you having a fun with Liss? Give her a kiss for me."

"Yeah. She's busy right now. What kind of kiss?"

"Ideally something sloppy, with tongue. But come back to the hotel first so I can watch."

"Pervert."

"Indeed."

I laughed and stepped outside the tattoo place. The guy at the counter had been glaring at me since I started talking.

"You going to do anything today?"

"Yes," Dex replied. "Wait for you to come back. I miss you."

"No you don't."

"Yes, I do. Come home. We'll go out on a date."

"A what?"

"Date. You know, eat dinner in a restaurant. I'll be nervous; you'll mess about with your hair. It'll be fun."

It hit me in that second that we never had actually been on a date. Sure, we'd shared a fair number of meals and all day together, but most of that was with everyone else. "I… really?"

"Yes, really. I'll make a reservation somewhere. If I can. Maybe I'll ask the concierge."

"Um…okay. I'll finish my outing with Liss and meet you at the hotel. Dinner around eight?"

"Got it. See you soon."

"Bye." I hung up the phone and just stood there for a while, smiling. Dex had asked me on a date. And he was going to plan it. My fears seemed a little silly, suddenly.

I was still over the moon happy when Liss emerged an hour later. She had a bandage over her ankle, but peeled it back to show me the tattoo. It was a tiny lightning bolt piercing a heart. "Cute," I told her. "What does it mean?"

She flashed a strange little smile and took my arm, leading me down the street. "Everything. It means everything."

FIVE

Getting ready for my date with Dex, I was ridiculously anxious. Choosing clothes was easy; I only had one really nice dress with me. It hung well on top, the clever folds balancing my shape, and skimming over my wide hips in a way I thought was fairly sexy. But I spent half an hour on my hair, knowing he'd love it down, but nervous that it looked messy.

By the time he knocked on my door I was ready, but still a little shaky. Any concerns about my appearance evaporated from my brain when I saw him. Dex was wearing a suit. A real one. No tie, but that just added to the look. He was rock and roll James Bond and I just stood there staring for a long time.

"Wow," I finally said.

He grinned and fussed with his slicked back hair. "And you." He kissed me lightly on the lips and I could feel the jitters in his body. He really was nervous, too. Somehow that comforted me.

"I'm ready if you are."

"Great." He grabbed my hand and led me out to the hallway.

"Gonna tell me where we're going?"

"Some fancy French place. Apparently you need reservations a month or two out, but the concierge here knows somebody."

"That sounds exciting."

He shrugged, pressing the button to call the elevator. "I certainly hope so. As good as you look right now, it's going to take a really amazing meal to make me happy I didn't lock your door behind us and stay in all night."

I blushed and looked down, happy that the elevator arrived quickly.

When we got downstairs there was a cab waiting for us, and in just a few minutes we were in front of the restaurant. It didn't really look like anything special, just a small sign and a somewhat modern-looking front window. Inside there was a tiny bar and a dozen or so tables, with a staircase leading up to a balcony. The décor was tasteful but opulent – something I'd noticed the French seemed to have perfected. Large gilt mirrors reflected the soft light around the room, bathing everything in a warm glow. The host greeted us and called Dex *Monsieur* Winters, which made both of us, laugh inappropriately.

We were seated at a table near the back. The host placed a single sheet of paper in front of Dex and then disappeared.

"What the hell is this?"

"What?" I craned my neck to look. "What does that say?"

Dex shrugged. "I think this is supposed to be the menu. But it's just three options and prices."

"Huh, weird. I guess they bring us whatever they want?"

"Oh boy. I hope we don't need to go out for a burger

after this."

I giggled, earning myself a stern look from the woman at the table next to us.

In a few minutes a waiter arrived and explained the process to us. Each item on the so-called menu was a different number of courses; the actual dishes were selected by the chef. Since neither of us had any food allergies, we just went for it. But after doing some quick math in my head, I realized our dinner, with wine, would cost more than a month's rent.

"Dex, this is too much," I whispered once we were alone again."

"Hush. Didn't you tell me earlier that I'm going to be a rich man?"

"Honey, you clear like a penny from that, if you're lucky."

He laughed. "Still. Just enjoy your dinner. Don't worry about the money."

"Okay."

We sipped wine and chatted about the people around us while waiting for the first course to arrive. I was feeling very sophisticated right until the waiter delivered a plate with a few tiny specs of food to each of us. He blathered on for a good five minutes in excellent English about the dish, but it seemed impossible that all of the things he mentioned were included in what amounted to nothing bigger than a two-bite brownie.

Dex and I exchanged a look and then dug in, briefly.

The rest of the meal continued the same way. Sometimes he brought us three plates with miniscule bits of food on them. At some point I lost track of how many things we ate, but my stomach told me they still hadn't amounted to a whole dinner yet.

The food was delicious, at least. And the wine lovely. But as we kept pecking at little fussy bits of whatever-the-hell, it got harder to keep from laughing. Especially when the chef himself came out to say hello and ask how we were enjoying the food. Dex was great, offering praise that sounded completely genuine. I just sat there smiling, trying not to embarrass myself. I realized this would be his life now, strangers of every stripe fawning over him while I watched, almost invisible.

Finally, when our trio of desserts was finished and the holy-shit size checked had been paid, we left, arm in arm. Outside we made it a few yards down the block before collapsing into a fit of hysterical laughter. My stomach was only half full, and all the wine had gone to my head.

Once he calmed down a bit, Dex wrapped his arms around my waist and kissed me softly.

"What was that for?"

"An apology."

"Why?"

"For taking you out to that ridiculous dinner. Next time we'll go someplace normal. With a real menu."

"You don't need to apologize. It was wonderful. Weird, and really not me, but wonderful. Anywhere I go with you is."

He smiled and kissed me again, this time deeper, probing. His whole body pressed insistently against mine and I let out a soft moan.

"Let's go home."

Dex smirked. "Yes. On to my favorite part of this date." He fisted his hand in my hair and pulled me even closer. I closed my eyes and inhaled, enjoying the scent of his skin, just as ready for what came next as he was.

WELL ROCKED

~ * ~

The next day I was still floating on a cloud. Dex and I had made love all night, but I didn't feel tired at all. I left Dex sleeping, grabbed a quick breakfast and then went over to the venue to meet Ryan.

When I got backstage was on the phone, so I ran through some now-automatic tasks, checking that everything would be ready for the show.

I waved at Red, who was wrangling his expanded security team, now that the guys were attracting so much media attention. He was in his customary t-shirt and black cargo pants, massive arms crossed, looking every inch the intimidating bodyguard.

He saw me and gestured for me to join them. I did, feeling ridiculously short among the big, brawny men.

"Becca, I'm glad you're here. Let me introduce you to my new crew." He recited a list of names, and I scrawled each one down in my notes, so I could be sure to remember them. Each of the five was more imposing than the last, but they smiled politely.

"Nice to meet you all. I'm sure Red has everything under control, but if you need anything, feel free to ask me."

Red grinned. "She means it, fellas. Becca keeps this crazy train running, don't let anyone tell you different."

I rolled my eyes. "Stop it. We all give one hundred percent."

"Well, your hundred is worth a lot more than some others." He arched an eyebrow and I realized he was talking about Mia. It was nice to see some of the team knew what she did to me and Dex, and didn't like it either.

After exchanging a few more pleasantries with Red, I

47

headed back to where I'd left Ryan. We had a long list of things to do, and the day was flying by.

I found him just hanging up.

"Good morning, Rebecca," he said.

"Hi Ryan."

"Did you enjoy your days off?"

I nodded. "Sure. Um…how about you?"

"I don't get days off." He sniffed. "While you and the boys have been enjoying Paris I've been working."

"Right, of course. Sorry," I muttered. He sure knew how to bring down a good mood. "Shall we get started?"

"Before we begin, there are a few things I need to discuss with you."

Oh boy, here we go. I braced myself for another lecture.

"First of all, I want to commend you for performing your required tasks adequately. I appreciate that you responded to my messages on your off days. As you know, this business never stops. And as things escalate, we all need to keep on top of things."

"Right. I mean, thank you." It wasn't exactly effusive praise, but I'd take it.

"Yes. Second issue, you should know Mia is leaving the tour."

My heart leapt a little. "She is?" I tried to ask evenly.

"Yes. She decided it was best. While she's an excellent member of the team, her dreams lie elsewhere."

"I see. What does this mean for the tour blog?"

"I'll be hiring someone new to be onboard by the time we get to Zurich hopefully, or Milan. In the meantime I'll need you to work on it. We won't have the video content, but you can use whatever you like from the official photographs."

That made sense. We hired a local photographer in

each city to get shots backstage at the venue and during the shows. All of their pictures were uploaded to a site we and the label could access for whatever promotional purposes were required. I didn't say it to Ryan, but the truth was Mia had been mostly using those for her infrequent posts anyway, on the blog and the band's Facebook page. In fact, I couldn't remember the last video she took, so no one would notice the difference. I wasn't particularly excited about adding a new task to my list, but considering I was still on "probation," there wasn't anything I could do about it. I'd just hope he got someone new quickly.

"Okay, great," I said, jotting down some information. "Is there anything else?"

"Yes. With sales of the album increasing and the attention the band is receiving, things are going to get even more hectic. You understand that, right?"

"Of course."

"I'll be calling on you more in the upcoming weeks. There are some high-level discussions going on that I can't disclose at this point. But I will say this. Work harder than you ever have before. Dream Defiled has limitless potential, and we're all going to do our parts to help them become the biggest band in the world."

My throat went dry. Not that I didn't want the guys to be successful. I did. But when I signed on I had no idea what the future might hold. And now that my feelings for Dex were getting deeper, it worried me a bit. The pressures and stresses super stardom created.

I'd seen so many friends of my dad, or groups he worked with go to the next level just to implode. I didn't want that for the band, and I feared how my lover might react. This group was his family. His everything. I silently hoped they could keep it together. Maintain the closeness that made them great together.

"All right. We only have a few hours left before sound check. Come with me," Ryan said.

I nodded and followed him back to the loading dock, but my mind was a million miles away. Fortunately, most of my tasks were easily performed without much attention. We went through the normal dramas, missing boxes, minor equipment damage, late staff, but things mostly ran smooth.

By the time the band arrived, we were ready for them. I had just finished correcting the venue's ridiculously wrong setup of the dressing room when the invasion began. After two days without work, everyone was full of energy. The guys seemed to be itching to play some music, so they dropped bags and clothes off and practically raced onstage to get going. I smiled, getting a quick wink from Dex before they left.

I arranged everything they'd dropped and then went out to watch from the floor of the club. I waved at the equipment tech, Steve, up at the sound board with the venue's technician.

Joe led the guys through a quick sound check, and I noticed Liss hadn't come over with them. I hoped she would show up later for the show. I wanted to thank her for the advice and see how her man had reacted to her new tattoo. I dashed off a text to her, checking in, and turned my attention back to the stage.

Of course, they sounded great. But in the middle of a song, I remembered that no one had made copies of the new set list. So instead of staying to listen, I had to run and find the manager of the venue to get it printed off and copied for the guys. It was a tiny oversight that only I knew about, but it bugged me. I was a little off my game at a time I really couldn't afford to be.

Luckily, the club's manager, *Arnaud*, was in his office and happy to help me. He was medium height and very slim, with a wild mop of curly black hair and a playful smile. His English wasn't great, but I couldn't complain since my French was abysmal. We communicated fine and he told me stories of disastrous shows and hilarious mishaps while I got the set lists together.

I was still giggling at one of his stories as I went back to the stage. The guys had cleared out, probably back to the dressing room to drink and eat. I placed a list at each designated place and was about to find Ryan when I saw Rick stomping over to his drum set. He crouched down as if searching for something

"Uh, hey. Is there anything you need?" I asked him cautiously.

"Not from you," he snarled.

"Okay." I shrugged it off, used to his terrible attitude.

He stood up, shoving what looked like a small scrap of fabric into the pocket of his jeans.

"Well, um…see you later." I headed past him to the wings, but he slid over to block my way.

"Hang on a sec."

I looked up into his cold, green eyes. "What is it?"

"There's something you need to know."

"All right." I glanced around, but no one was in sight.

"Look at me when I'm talking to you."

I met his gaze, narrowing my eyes.

"Nice. I knew it."

"Knew what? Stop talking in riddles."

"You're a bitch, you know that?"

I gasped. "Excuse me?"

"You heard me. Don't try that little miss innocent act on me. I see through you. You think because you're back

51

that you're untouchable. But I didn't want you back. We don't need you."

"I…" I paused. "Look, you don't have to like me. I don't care. But I'm just here to do my job. If you stay out of my way I'll stay out of yours."

"But you don't," he spat. "You're always around. Distracting Dex, trying to turn him into the same pussy-whipped sack of shit Joe is lately. This is by band and these are my guys. The last thing we need is a bunch of homely sluts hanging on."

Without thinking I reared back and slapped him across the face. The sound echoed in the quiet club and we both froze with shock.

"Truth hurts, sweetheart?"

I bristled at his voice, dripping with sarcasm. "This conversation is over. Let me by."

"You go when I say you go. Hit me all you want. But it won't change the fact that you're nothing to us. They all bent over backwards to keep you around, but it had nothing to do with *you*. That was about Dex. Because he's a breakdown waiting to happen.

"No one stood up when my girl got fired for doing exactly the same thing. Because I'm a grown ass man. I handle my problems instead of drowning them in liquor."

I dimly recalled hearing that the girl who had my job before me had been let go when Ryan found out she'd had a fling with Rick. Honestly, I couldn't imagine anyone wanting to get anywhere near him. And sure, it was unfair. But that wasn't my fault.

"You say you guys are so close, then why are you talking about Dex light that?"

"Because I know who he really is. And it isn't the same guy playing house with you right now. What are you going to do when he implodes? Bring him a cookie? What about when he gets tired of looking at your fat ass and dealing with your boring personality? You still gonna be fetching beers when he's banging supermodels every night? Gonna deliver condoms to his room and wade through the groupies?"

A war was happening inside my head. Part of me wanted to slap him again. A lot. Just wail on him for being such an asshole. But his words stung, too. Hurt me somewhere deep inside that I had been struggling to hide. Tears pricked at my eyes and I fled, shoving past him to escape. I wouldn't let him see me cry, couldn't give him the satisfaction, but I couldn't stop it from happening.

I hid out from everyone for the rest of the afternoon and evening. When the guys headed out for dinner I just pretended to be busy, found an empty room, and sat there alone. I'd never experienced such a roller coaster of emotions in one day and it exhausted me. I dozed off in a chair, surrendering to the calm of oblivion.

By the time I re-emerged, it was time for the show and no one seemed to notice my mood. I kept my distance from everyone, even Dex. And when we all went back to the hotel, I squeezed his arm and said goodnight in the hallway, not giving him a chance to question why, or ask me to join his plan to hit some bars with the others.

SIX

The next day there wasn't time for talking to Dex or anything but work. The guys had interviews all day and then the night off. The next day was our last show in Paris. I had a ton of work, including untangling the mess Mia had made of the band's online presence. I was tucked away in a corner of the suite we'd rented to host the journalists, trying to concentrate on what was in front of me. But Rick's words kept playing over and over in my head and I found myself staring at the guys as they chatted and posed for photos.

Joe, as always, was the consummate professional. He charmed everyone, commanding the room. But I could see a bit of strain around his eyes. Probably because Liss would be going back to the States in a few days. I was going to miss her too, so he must have been crushed. Even though we weren't halfway through the tour yet, it felt like an ending.

Dex and Matthew were huddled close. An unlikely pair, from physical to personality differences, their closeness was obvious. Dex seemed to bring the shorter man out of his shell a bit, and Matthew inspired a sweet, protective side of Dex.

And then there was Rick. Standing apart from the others, he only engaged a reporter when asked a specific question, and his face never cracked a smile for a photograph. I wondered why he was even in the band if everything made him so angry.

I frowned and turned my attention back to the work I was doing. Ryan had charged me with working harder, and I was going to do just that. Push away my own confusion and get things in order. I needed to prove to him that I could rise to the challenge. And I needed to prove to myself that no matter what happened, I could do my job and do it well.

And somewhere, in the middle of lists and calls and everything else, I stopped thinking about my problems and just enjoyed doing what I liked. From an early age, maybe as a response to the chaos of the creative-types surrounding me, I loved organizing things. Closets, boxes, books, anything. When I had nightmares, instead of crawling into bed with my father, I'd go into his home studio and arrange sheet music and his files.

Then, after he had the stroke, there was so much to do. A house to clean and organize. Boxes in the house, the garage, a storage facility. I whipped through it all, Getting his life in order while my heart ached with worry.

Even when he'd gone into the care home, I made sure his room was perfectly arranged. Selling the house had provided more distractions that appealed to my meticulous nature. Selling things, donating others, keeping a few mementos, I'd spend hours going through the remnants of his old life. Remembering good times and bad. Crying alone, surrounded by my past.

Maybe it was obsessive or weird, but I was good at

keeping things together, even when I was falling apart. I'm sure a psychologist would say I was hiding from my feelings, but sometimes you just have to find a way through. Sometimes coping is the best you can hope for.

And now, on the tour, cope is what I did. Through the busy day into the evening when the rest of the band left and I was alone with Dex.

I didn't tell him about my argument with Rick. I didn't say a word about my fears. I just kissed him and took his hand, letting him lead me out into Paris. It was our last night, and I wanted to enjoy it. Even more, I wanted him to enjoy it.

We had dinner at a lovely bistro. The menu was two pages and the food filled the plates. Afterwards, he surprised me with tickets to the Eiffel Tower. For the first time that day, I was truly excited. We hurried through the streets to make our time. They had a very strict set of rules and I didn't want to risk missing a trip to the top.

In line with our group, a pair of women recognized Dex. Fortunately, they just said hello and didn't make a scene. He took one picture with them and then we were alone again.

Once we got to the top of the tower, I wouldn't have cared if the entire world came up to him. I was mesmerized by the city below us. Lights dotting the landscape as far as I could see. The majestic and historic beauty visible from every angle.

Dex came up behind me and put his arms around my waist. "Are you happy?"

"Very," I replied.

"I'm glad. You've been quiet today, a bit somber."

"Just tired, I guess. But this…this is perfect. Invigorating."

"Good. I want to make you happy, Becca."

I turned around in his arms. "You do."

He leaned down and kissed me. In the middle I jumped away and squealed.

"What? What's wrong?"

"Wrong? Nothing!" I flung my arms wide. "I'm kissing the sexiest man I've ever met at the top of the Eiffel Tower. It's so nuts."

He laughed, as did a few other people nearby.

I grinned sheepishly. "Sorry, it just hit me. My life is amazing." I grabbed Dex and kissed him again. He pulled me close and drove his tongue deep inside my mouth. I gripped his back, nearly climbing his body in my haste to get even closer. Paris and people and lights disappeared. All that existed in that perfect moment was us.

When our time slot ended, we took the elevator back down to the ground and found a cab to take us back to the hotel. On the way, I couldn't keep my hands off of him. From shoving my hands up the front of his shirt to climbing atop him in the back of the cab, I was completely out control.

The driver mentioned something about the romance of Paris getting to us, and I agreed, giddy. But it wasn't just the city. It was Dex. He scared me and thrilled me in equal measure, and for once, I was just going to let whatever happened happen. I wanted him, needed him. And for the time being, I had him.

And so, when we finally got back to my room, I took full advantage. Throwing off my clothes quickly, I climbed up into bed and gestured for him to join me. The look of amusement on his face shifted to desire when I slid my hand over the growing bulge in his pants.

"Whatever is making you act like this, please tell me so

I can bring you twice as much every day."

I chuckled low in my throat and straddled him. "Shut up, Dex."

He did, lowering his mouth to my neck and then my breasts, nipping and licking. I moaned and writhed on him, letting myself get lost in the sensations completely, as if, somewhere deep down, I knew the time for such care-free passion was about to end.

The two weeks passed so quickly I barely noticed. After all the drama, things were finally settling down, or so it seemed. We left Paris and managed to get to Zurich, Milan and then Vienna for shows without any catastrophic weather or personnel changes.

By the time we arrived in Munich for another set of two concerts, Dex and I were closer than ever, and managing to find a comfortable balance between spending time together and getting tired of looking at each other. Some nights he'd go out with the group and I'd stay at the hotel. He'd come home and we'd cuddle or make love, just enjoying our time. Other nights we'd both hit the town, checking out a combination of tourist spots and cool placed recommended by locals. In every city the crowds were bigger, the lines longer.

Paparazzi were stationed outside the venues to get look at the band. And when the album was officially certified platinum and the guys hit the cover of a huge music magazine, suddenly there were photographers inside the hotels, sometimes even trying to sneak into the rooms we rented.

It was a kind of controlled madness, really. Under-fed and sleep-deprived, we moved across Europe in a daze. I was more tired than I'd ever been in my life, but found it difficult to just go to sleep at night. It seemed like there was too much to do, too many things to see and experience to waste precious moments with my eyes closed.

In fact, the only time we stopped running around was when, late at night, Dex and I would lock ourselves up in our hotel room for some privacy. We'd long since stopped bothering to get separate rooms.

The night after the first show in Munich we all went out to say goodbye to Liss. When we boarded a plane to Copenhagen, she'd be heading in the opposite direction, back to the States to get ready to start school in the fall.

It was a bittersweet night. Everyone was on their best behavior. Rick came for one drink and then left, thankfully. Even Ryan stopped by for a toast before going off to do whatever he did during downtime.

But the rest of the gang, of my strange little road family stayed together. Patrick, the new social media person Ryan hired, took what felt like hundreds of pictures and videos of us. We got drunker and louder and more loving by the hour until the owner of the bar had to ask us to leave.

Laughing amiably, we piled into cars and went back to the hotel, ending up in one room, ordering room service and keeping the party going until the sun came up. I was happy. Really happy, though it was sad to lose my closest friend in the group. Liss had become a confidant. We were very different, but in similar situations, and sometimes felt like outsiders, but we always had each other. Once she was gone I'd be the only girl on the tour. When I hugged her goodnight, it was really goodbye, and I shed a few tears. She punched me in the arm and reminded me it wasn't forever.

We'd call and email, and when the band went back to the US, we'd see each other frequently.

I was still feeling a little sad when Dex and I fell into bed.

"You okay, love?"

"Yeah. It just feels like…I don't know. Like something is ending for real."

"You mean Liss? Don't worry. She can't stay away long. When we get back she'll visit. And then before you know it we'll be out on tour again. Joe won't go too many days without his girl." He kissed my shoulder. "And I finally understand why. I don't know what I'd do without seeing your face every day."

I smiled. "Yeah, yeah. You're so smooth."

He winked and pulled me close. "Go to sleep. Nothing will be different in the morning. The world keeps turning and you're my girl."

That was a lovely thought to drift off to as rays of morning sun peaked through the closed drapes.

But Dex was wrong. Everything was different in the morning.

SEVEN

S leeping in was a rare pleasure for me. While the guys could party all night and then roll out of bed early the next afternoon, I usually had too much to do to get away with that. Besides, my brain has a nasty habit of waking me up with thoughts of tasks to complete and lists to build.

But this morning I managed to stay wrapped in Dex's arms, sleeping away until my cell phone rang, waking me. I untangled myself from his grasp and grabbed the phone where it sat charging by the bed.

"Hello…"

"Is this Rebecca Hall?" a soft, British-accented voice asked.

"Yes, this is Becca."

"Ah, yes. So sorry. Becca, I don't know if you recall meeting me. I'm Karen, Dexter's aunt."

I shook my head a few times to clear it, and blinked. "Karen, of course. Hi. Um…are you looking for Dex? I can give you his number."

"No, dear. I'm calling to speak with you." Her voice was very serious. I looked at Dex, but he was still fast asleep. Climbing out of bed, I crept into the bathroom.

"Is something wrong?"

"I'm rather afraid so. This isn't the kind of thing to share over the phone, but I wanted him to know as soon as possible."

My heart sank, and I knew what she was going to say before she spoke again.

"Allen passed away last night. It was peaceful and painless. I was there with him. Dexter should know that. His father wasn't alone." Her voice cracked.

"Karen, I'm so sorry for your loss."

"Thank you, dear. Listen, I'm telling you because I know you're close with my nephew. I could see it when you were here at the hospital visiting. He's going to need you now. Allen wasn't a perfect man, and he was a rubbish father. I know that. But he loved my sister and he loved his son as best he was able."

"Of course he did," I whispered, heart breaking for Dex. "I'm glad you called me. I'll tell him, and have him contact you, okay?"

"Yes. There are arrangements to make, of course. I can handle most of it, but he should be involved."

"Yeah. And I can help too."

"There's one more thing, dear."

"Yes?"

"A reporter came to the hospital a couple of days ago asking questions. Wanted to know if they had the right Allen Winters. So now that he's gone, I expect they'll find out soon."

"Yes, you're probably right. Look, if someone bothers you, just have them call the band's press team. You don't have to say anything. You've got enough to handle right now."

"Thank you, dear."

"Anytime. Hold on, let me get you the number." I scrolled through to find it and rattled it off to her. "If there's anything else you need, feel free to call me. I'm going to wake Dex up now."

"All right."

I thought for a moment. "Karen, you know, I have an idea. You're Dex's family. I think he should hear this from you. Stay on the phone and I'll get him. Then I'm still here to help him cope, but the news should come from you."

"What a good idea. You're a very thoughtful young woman." Her words almost made me smile. Karen was middle-age at the oldest, but talked to me like she was a hundred years older than me. It was oddly sweet.

I walked back into the bedroom. Dex was still sleeping, now on his back with an arm flung across my side of the bed. I sat down next to him and held his hand. "Honey, wake up."

He grunted a few times and rolled away from me. I spoke again, this time squeezing his fingers. That worked. He turned his head back to face me and blinked a few times.

"Becca? What's going on? It can't be time for the show yet."

"Not yet. But I've got an important call for you. I need you to get up."

The corner of one of his lips quirked up. "I can get up for you anytime." He reached out a hand to touch me, but then his eyes widened as he looked at my face. "Something's wrong."

I nodded and he sat up, back against the pillows and headboard. "Tell me."

I handed the phone over and stood up, giving him a tiny bit of space.

"Hello?"

I could track the words his aunt must be saying by the expression on his face. First confusion, then shock, then... something I couldn't recognize.

"Yes, thank you," he said before handing the phone back to me.

"Karen?" I asked, but there was no sound.

"She's gone," Dex said. "And so is he. One from the phone the other from the world." His voice was flat, his face now impassive.

"Dex, honey. I'm so sorry." I put the phone down and reached out to him. "Do you want to talk?"

He stared at me for a long moment. "Right now I want to take a piss."

"I-uh-okay." I stood there silently as he rose and went into the bathroom. I thought maybe he wanted some time alone, but he came back quickly.

"Since I'm up, do you want to get some breakfast?"

"Dex..."

"What?"

"I...your father died last night. You just want to go eat breakfast?"

"Will not eating breakfast bring him back to life?"

"No, of course not. That isn't what I meant."

He sighed, rubbing his head. "I know. Becca, stop looking at me like that."

"Like what?"

"Like I'm some kind of rabid wild animal you best be wary of. I'm fine."

"How can you be fine?"

"I just am. I'm not you. I don't have all this unresolved

shit about my father. I said goodbye to him when we visited. That was enough. I didn't expect to ever see him again, and now I know I never will. End of the story."

"I don't believe you really feel that way."

His jaw tightened. "Don't tell me how I feel."

"I'm not!" I paled. "I'm sorry; I don't know what the right thing to say is."

Dex walked over to me and put his hands on my shoulders. "You don't need to say anything. In fact, maybe we shouldn't talk at all. If you want to make me feel better, there are other ways." His hands slipped over my shoulders and down my back.

I stepped out of the embrace. "Dex, I don't think this is the right time for sex."

His voice went low and sensual. "It is always the right time for sex." He looked down my body in a way that made me want to cover myself, even though I was in pajamas.

"Stop it, please."

"Why? Don't play the blushing virgin with me. That ship has sailed, as they say."

"Dex," I gasped.

"Come on. Don't you want me?" He sidled closer again, this time tucking a thumb under my chin to make me look into his face.

"That's not the issue. I just think we should talk. Or maybe I should leave you alone."

"Bullshit, Becca."

"What?"

His other hand grabbed my wrist. "You asked what to do to help me and I told you. But if you're going to go back to being a prude, you can just go ahead and fuck off."

I blinked back tears, the pain where he squeezed my wrist nothing in comparison to the pain in my heart. I yanked away from his grasp and fumbled over to grab some clothes. "I-I'll just give you some time."

"Whatever," he drawled before going back into the bathroom, slamming the door behind him.

"Well," I said to the empty room. "That went well."

I changed quickly, grabbed my phone, and headed out. I wouldn't let myself think about the things Dex had said to me. It was grief, and him trying to avoid whatever feelings were churning up inside him.

I walked down the hall and knocked on Ryan's door. He answered, phone in hand.

"Rebecca, what is it?"

"Sorry to both you, but I just got the news. Dex's father died."

"Oh. That's terrible. How is he doing?"

I shrugged. "Denial right now, I think. I would have let him tell you, but I assume we need as much lead time as possible to cancel tonight's show. I don't know when the service will be yet, but he's going to need a while to recover and also deal with logistics."

"Let me stop you right there. I know whatever relationship you have with Dex is close. But I've known him for years. He's not going to want to cancel. Being on stage will help him get through this."

"I-Ryan, I don't mean to be rude, but he needs to take some time to deal with this."

"That isn't your decision to make, is it?"

"No. Of course not. I'm just trying to do the right thing for him."

He snorted. "You mean the thing you want him to do."

"No." Tears stung my eyes again. "Look, whatever Dex decides, I'll support. I just thought you should know."

"Yes, fine. Thanks for informing me."

"Sure. But listen, if-"

I never got a chance to finish that thought before he shut the door in my face.

"Zero for two," I muttered, heading back to our room.

But when I went inside, it was empty. The bathroom, too, and I saw Dex's shoes were gone from the floor where he'd kicked them off. Since Ryan's room was in the opposite direction from the elevators, it would have been easy for Dex to leave while I was down there.

Unsure what to do, I pulled our suitcases out of the closet. Whether he decided to go back to Bristol or on to Copenhagen, we'd be flying out the next day, and I might as well get some things ready.

I packed up the room, took a shower and got dressed, and had two cups of coffee, and Dex still hadn't returned. I sent him a text message and decided to get to work instead of sitting around worrying.

By the time I had to get over to the club, I'd spent a lot of time doing not much of anything, and felt worse than before. I had no idea where Dex was, or if he'd even turn up for the show.

I managed to grab Matthew and we shared a cab over to the venue so we could talk privately.

"I assume you heard the news," I said.

"Yeah. It's sad."

"Right. Well, have you talked to Dex today? He's not returning my calls or messages."

He shook his head. "Mine either."

"I'm worried. Are you?"

Matthew shrugged. "Not sure."

"Okay." This might have been our longest conversation to date, but he wasn't being helpful at all. "I'm going to keep calling him. You let me know if you hear anything?"

"Sure."

I sighed and turned to look out the window. When we arrived at the club we went inside together and then split up. Matthew waited for the rest of the band by the stage, and I scampered over to check in with Ryan.

A while later sound check had come and gone without Dex, and no one I asked had heard from him at all. I was starting to freak out. Ryan was pissed and the club's manager livid, but I was just worried. Dex was out there somewhere, alone, in a city where he didn't know anybody, thinking and feeling who knows what. I wanted to be able to help him, hold him. Get through this together. But I couldn't do that if I couldn't find him.

I left the venue for a few minutes, heading down the street to a little coffee shop we'd found the day before. I ordered a drink and waited for it to be prepared, turning my attention to the television. Because most of the patrons were going to the show, it was showing the English news channel. And a story about Dex's father's death.

"My god," I whispered. Now the whole world would know, and poor Dex hadn't had a moment to deal with it. The story speculated whether or not the tour would end, if this loss would ruin the band's trajectory. Like any of that mattered. I was fuming and sipping my coffee when my phone rang. I looked at the number and was disappointed to see it was Ryan.

"Hello?"

"Get back here, Rebecca. Your boyfriend has finally arrived."

I almost yelled with relief. "Be there in a minute."

I ran back to the club, barely giving the door guy time to check my all-access pass. At full speed I went to the dressing rooms and found the whole band surrounded a prone form on the floor. Dex.

"What happened?" A million terrible possibilities flashed through my mind.

Rick grunted. "Nothing. He's just drunk off his ass."

"Shit."

"Yeah."

I went into automatic problem-solving mode. "Okay, everyone leave us alone for a minute. I need ice-cold water and a gallon of coffee."

Joe shoved the other guys out of the room and then came back in. "Whatever you're gonna do, hurry. We told Ryan Dex got here, but didn't mention what state he's in."

"Got it. Thank you."

He nodded, looked at me with pity, and left.

I slid down to the floor, raising Dex's head to rest in my lap. The stench of liquor on him made me a little queasy, but it didn't matter.

"Dex," I said loudly, shaking his arm. "Dex, can you hear me?"

He groaned softly, but didn't open his eyes. I scanned down his body and saw a few scrapes and tears, as if he'd fallen down quite a bit. Worried about a concussion, I dug gently through his dark hair, but didn't feel any bumps or signs of bruising.

Apparently my touch helped, though. His eyes fluttered open and then squinted. "Too bright."

I let out a panicked laugh. He spoke. That was a really good sign.

"Honey, you really scared me. Where have you been all

day?"

"Drinking."

"That much I could tell. Where?"

"Everywhere. You'd be surprised how many places there are to get drunk in the middle of the day. And now that I'm a celebra-cebret-*shit*, famous guy, lots of people bought me drinks."

Now that he was safe, and generally okay, I let the anger I'd been holding back spring to the surface. "Well that's lovely. So glad you had a nice day. But you've got a show in less than an hour. And everyone's been worried sick."

He sat up quickly, but then leaned against me as his face went green and his eyes unfocused. "Don't want worry. I'm fine. How many fucking times do I have to tell you I'm fine?"

"This is fine? You're completely wasted. I don't even know how you got here."

"Simple. I…well, I'm not sure. But I'm here. Ready to rock and roll." He cackled, and then held a hand up to his forehead. "Ouch."

I pushed him so he rested against the wall instead of me, and got up. "You're being such an asshole right now."

"So what? My father is dead. I can be an arse, asshole if I want."

"That's true. But I don't have to stand here and watch you do it."

"You wouldn't leave me."

"I will. When you're ready to talk and deal with this, I'll be there. But I won't stand by while you drink yourself into oblivion."

"Bull. You won't go because you love me and you know I need you."

I wanted to punch him. And hug him. And tell him,

70

"Yes, I do love you, but I hate you right now."

But I didn't do any of those things. I put my cup of coffee down on the table and walked out the door without saying a word.

Outside I ran into Matthew. He was holding a whole carafe of coffee and a few bottles of water.

I smiled at him. "Thank you. Take that in to him if you want. I need a break."

"Okay. Hey, wait a second."

I turned around. "What is it?"

"He's crazy in love with you. Whatever happens, don't give up on him."

Shaking my head, I sighed and continued down the hallway.

Calling the fact that Dex managed to play the show a miracle felt like the understatement of my life. His performance was far from perfect, but some combination of a little sleep, a lot of coffee, and the deafening noise sobered him up enough to get through the set without embarrassing himself. I watched from the wings, holding my breath most of the time.

Most shows Dex was magnetic and constantly in motion. Playing off of Joe and the others, drawing the audience into his music effortlessly. This time was different. He got through the songs fine, but there was no action. He stood in one spot and connected with no one. But considering the state I'd found him in, it was a triumph of professionalism. Relatively speaking.

Once the encore was over, he headed out the back and

71

into the waiting van. I made eye contact with Ryan to make sure he saw I was leaving too, and followed.

"Jesus, please not another lecture," Dex said darkly as I climbed up and sat next to him.

"I just wanted to see how you're feeling."

"Terrible. But I'll get a few shots in me and be fine."

"Don't you think a good night's sleep would be better?"

"Bloody hell, Becca. Don't you ever let up?"

I gritted my teeth but didn't speak.

Dex groaned, pushed past me, and walked out of the van. He took a few steps and then turned back. "A million times I've told you you're not on duty with me. I don't need you to organize me, fix me. Why can't you just *be* with me?"

"I can. But this isn't you."

"What if it is?"

"Then I've been fighting to make us work for no reason. I know you're hurting, but digging yourself a deeper hole isn't going to help. You need to talk. To be surrounded with people who love you. You have to let us in."

He stared at me, and for a second his eyes softened. But just as quickly, they went cold again. "Not tonight I don't," he said, and walked away. It was becoming a pattern with us, and one I didn't care for one bit.

EIGHT

I didn't wait up for him that night. And in the morning, when it was time to go to the airport, I didn't expect him to show, and he didn't. A part of me worried if he was dead in a ditch somewhere, but I knew he wasn't. He was either still drinking, or sleeping it off somewhere.

After making sure everyone else was prepared for the flight and saying a real goodbye to Liss, I took Ryan aside. For once, he actually listened to what I had to say.

"Are you sure this is the right course of action?"

I nodded. "I have to try, at least."

"All right. I'm trusting you with this. Keep me posted and we'll work out the details."

"Thank you, Ryan. For believing me."

"I may not agree with all of your choices, Rebecca. But I acknowledge you know what you're doing. So do it."

"I will."

He sighed and turned to get in the vehicle with the others. I stood in front of the hotel, watching as the van pulled away, and then went back upstairs.

A few hours later the door opened and Dex came in.

"Why are you still here?" he asked.

"Waiting for you."

"I didn't ask you to do that."

"No, you didn't. Just like you didn't ask me to smooth things over with Ryan and the other members of your band. But I did that too. Or assure your aunt that you'd be in touch soon. But I did."

"Why?"

"Because I'm stupid. And a fool. I love you and there's nothing I won't do to help you, even when you won't help yourself."

He pulled a bottle of something out of a pocket and took a swig. "Fuck, who knew when my mother died I'd get another."

"I'm not trying to mother you. I'm just giving you one last chance to keep from messing up your whole life in a way you can't fix."

"You don't know anything about my life."

"Fuck you, Dex. I know everything about your life. I am here. I have been here."

"Maybe I don't want you here."

"Then tell me to go. Break up with me."

"No!"

I approached him. "Why?"

"I don't know. I…I don't want you gone. I just want you to stop."

"Stop what?"

"Stop caring so much. Stop trying to make me well. I'm not. I'm sick. Poisoned from birth and slowly dying. And you can't make that different. All you do is push and pull me, make me love you, need you. Make me want to be better. Be something you deserve. But I can't."

74

He slammed a flat palm against the wall.

"I can't be anything but this. I'm a fuck-up. All I've ever been good at, aside from fucking up, is music. I can sing and play and write. So that's what I do. And I'm good at it. But I'm not a good man and I never will be." A sob escaped him and he turned away.

I went over and put my hand on his shoulder, turning him around. "Don't say that, Dex. You're just in a bad place right now."

"Not just now. Always. My whole life. And I won't let you fall into this pit with me. I can't. You're the most wonderful thing in this fucking wasteland of a world and I won't be what ruins you, too."

I took his hand and dragged him over to the bed. We sat down. "How long have you felt this way?"

"Since the first time I saw you. God knows I tried to stay away. To let you be. But how could I? I'm weak. And I crave you like a drug, Becca. I live for the way your hair smells and how your hands feel on me. How your smile lights up a room and your voice reverberates through my bones. I'm hooked on every word you say. Every look you give me is a fix. I'm not strong enough to stay away from you. And you're so brave."

His fingers graze my cheek.

"I need you to end this. Get away from me before it's too late."

Through the tears streaming down my face I smiled. "I won't."

"Please. I'm begging you. I'll never be happy without you but I won't let you be miserable with me."

"Dex, you're an idiot," I said softly. "These weeks with you have been the happiest of my life. I spent so much time just going through the motions. Doing what I know, and getting by. All the pleasure and pain of this – us – has brought me to life. I wouldn't trade any of it. And as long as you care about me, I'm not giving up on you. Or on us."

His shoulders began to shake, and he cried in earnest, collapsing against me. I wrapped my arms around the strong body that had held me, and curled up with him, limbs entwined, faces inches apart while he wept.

I have no idea how long we stayed there like that. Only that when Dex finally sat up, my legs and arms ached from being in the same position so long. He gathered me close again and cupped my face in his hands.

"I don't know how to do this, Becca."

"Do what?"

"Live a real life. Face my issues. I only know how to hide. But I've never been able to hide from you. You see me."

"I do. Better than you see yourself. You're not weak, Dex. You're scared. But I know you can get through this. Get better."

"See, that's what scares me. The faith you have in me. I can't stand to think about disappointing you. Hurting you."

"You've already done both. But I'm still here. Shit, Dex. We're both a mess of bad histories and unsure futures. I don't know if that's something we can ever overcome completely. But I do know my life is better with you in it. And I know I'm willing to try, if you are."

"I am. I think. It's just…"

"Tell me."

"When we first got together, it felt like magic. Like I could be that guy, the one you see. But before long I was fucking up again. And that look on your face. It killed me. And so I just fucked up more. It's all I know how to do."

"No it isn't. You know how to be kind, and sweet and

make me feel like the most beautiful woman in the world. Those are superpowers, Dex. Not traits of a fuck-up."

"But what if I fail? What if I bollocks it all up again?"

"Then we'll fight. Yell, maybe not talk for a few days. But as long as we're both alive there's a chance to make it right."

He nodded. "Damn, you're really smart."

"I know. So listen to me, okay?"

"Okay."

I kissed his cheek and gripped one of his big hands between mine. "When I took this job, I was just hoping to work. Make some money and get back into the business that's in my blood. I know you understand that. But touring with you guys, and falling in love with you changed all that. Just doing the job isn't enough for me anymore. I don't need everything to be orderly and on schedule. There are more important things than that."

"Like what?"

"Like waking up next to you. The way your mouth feels against mine. How romantic it was to look out over all of Paris with you. How ridiculous that fancy dinner was. Every adventure I have, whether it is sitting at a café with Liss or meeting strangers on the street or just ordering room service with you.

"All of my lists are fine for work. But life isn't pages of things to check off. It's every experience, good and bad. Everything that brought us to this moment right here and everything we do after."

"What will that be?"

"I have no idea. But I know I want to find out with you by my side."

"That does sound good."

"I think so."

"How did I get so lucky that you came into my life?"

"I wonder the same thing about you every day. Even when I want to strangle you."

"You're an angel, Becca."

"No, I'm not. I'm a self-conscious weirdo with giant thighs and a tendency towards being anal-retentive."

"I like your thighs."

"That's because you're insane."

Dex laughed, and his smile stretched wide across his face.

"Feeling better?"

"A bit. But I'm still not sure what to do next. I know I have to deal with stuff and my dad. But I don't know how. Go back there? Pack up his place? Plan a funeral?"

"Yes, all of those things. But you don't have to do them alone."

"Aunt Karen is a nice lady, but I barely know her."

"I'm talking about me."

"No, I can't ask that of you."

"What part of 'in this together' did you not understand?"

"But, in order to do all of this, I have to leave the tour. Probably miss the rest of the dates over here."

"I know."

"But…your job?"

"Right now my job is getting you well. Supporting you through this process, whatever that means."

"Like a project?"

"No. Like family. You said I was part of the family, so *let me be* part of the family and help you."

"But Ryan and the guys…the other cities."

"Will all understand. It's all over the news that your father is gone. Besides, there are only three more shows. You've gone one man down because of illness before. This is no different."

"So we have time."

"Yes."

"It's kind of scary, this doing the right thing business."

I smiled. "I know. But nothing's so bad we can't beat it. Not your demons. Not the weather in Scotland. Or Ryan and Rick. Nothing."

Dex kissed me lightly and then rolled us over so he was on top of me. "Can we stop talking now?"

I laughed and wrapped my arms around his neck. "Yes, please."

He bent his head to my neck and kissed it tenderly before pulling back long enough to slide down my body a little. Pushing my shirt up, he planted another kiss on my bellybutton and then moved back towards my breasts. Cupping them in his hands, he bent to run his tongue along the edge of my bra, where satin met skin.

I shuddered and hooked my legs around his, pressing us closer together.

Dex chuckled, a low masculine sound, and flicked the clasp to release my breasts. Chest heaving, I shut my eyes. He sucked one pebbled tip into his mouth, taking long, slow draws that I could feel from the tip of my toes to the top of my head.

Not content to only drive me half mad, he reached between us and pushed his hand down between my legs. Even with the denim of my jeans between my damp flesh and his gifted fingers, I arched my back from the pleasure, spurring him on faster.

Dex took the hint, wordlessly doing exactly what I needed. In life he might be a mess, but in bed he was sure and perfect.

But as his fingers worked to open my jeans, I stopped

him. "Let's take this slow, okay?"

He nodded and sat back on his heels, lifting the t-shirt over his head and throwing it far away. His eyes glittered with desire as I saw up and took my shirt off too, dropping my bra onto the floor.

Dex got off me long enough to help pull down my pants and underwear before getting himself naked too.

Not long ago I would have been embarrassed, or at least a bit shy for him to see me completely naked in the light of the room, but that meant nothing anymore. Dex had seen into my soul, and let me see his. A flabby tummy and cellulite were inconsequential in the face of that depth of connection.

Besides, the look on his face as his gaze caressed every inch of me was intoxicating. He didn't see the flaws I did. Well, he saw the same parts, but instead of thinking them as imperfections, he adored them.

As if confirming that fact, he ran long fingers up from my ankle, sliding over my calf and knee, skimming and squeezing my thighs lightly, reverently. I sighed and lay back, spreading myself open for him with complete trust.

"What happened to slow?"

"There's slow and there's teasing. Don't tease me."

He laughed and pulled me up to a sitting position. "Nope. You said slow, you're getting slow."

I flashed a fake frown that turned to a very real smile when he buried his hands in my hair and pulled me in for a kiss. It was warm and sweet, deep and soulful. The softness of his lips and smooth slide of his tongue entranced me and all I could do was try to keep up. Dex was master of my body, every response and reaction, and I loved it.

But when I felt the brush of his erection, I realized slow wasn't going to cut it. So, with a devilish grin, I pushed him back so our positions were reversed, and settled myself between his legs. The muscles in his thighs tightened as my hair brushed them. I exhaled, blowing a puff of air across the wide tip of his member and watched it lengthen before my eyes.

I wrapped my fingers around the base and took the dusky head into my mouth.

Dex made a tight hissing sound that made me smile. He wasn't the only one who could tease.

With slow, lazy rolls of my tongue and gentle suction, I pleasured him, using the sounds he made, and ways his body reacted to guide me. Having him prone beneath me, leaving the care of his most intimate flesh entirely to me felt powerful, and I relished it.

But eventually, after a long time, he'd had enough. Dex grabbed my arms and scooted away. "I need you," he said. And in those three words I heard a world of things. The physical, the sexual, the emotional.

"Yes."

He grabbed a condom and rolled it down the thick column of flesh before lifting me above him.

"Like this?" I asked. "I'll smoosh you."

"Shut up, Becca."

I shut up. Not because he told me to, but because when the tip of him brushed my core I couldn't remember how to think, let alone speak. He pulled my hips down, sliding deep inside me, filling me. The tight fit was slicked by my arousal and I groaned ecstatically.

"Look at me," Dex ordered, and I did. Our eyes locked together as he began to move, guiding my body in time with his, slowly, gently, deliciously. And when he was all the way inside, and our bodies were joined completely, I placed my hands on the flat muscles of his chest, smiled, and let my hair fall forward into his face.

Dex chuckled and I felt it through our connected flesh. I braced myself on my hands and lifted up, before crashing back down again, taking my own breath away. It was intense and ridiculously erotic.

I repeated the maneuver and Dex flexed his hips to drive deeper, eliciting a tiny scream from me. He reached up and took one of my nipples between two fingers, tweaking the tender skin, heightening my pleasure even more.

Then, just as I felt the stirring in me that signaled an impending climax, he managed to grip me tight and flip us back, so I was beneath him now.

I gasped and he thrust again, the new angle sending me rocketing away. As I rode the waves of my orgasm, he never stopped, plunging in again and again, grinding against me, extending my climax forever, or so it felt.

And when he finally reached his own peak, our gazes locked on each other again, I knew once and for all that everything we'd been through together was worth it. He was still damaged and I was still troubled, but the connect we shared, that blossomed into love, was strong enough to make it through. I believed that with all of my heart, and couldn't have conjured up a doubt if I wanted to.

But wrapped in his strong arms, knowing that we would always have our struggles, I realized being there for each other made us both better. It's safe to fall apart when there's someone there to put you back together again. It was a luxury neither of us had grown up with, but a necessity I knew we could become accustomed to.

NINE

Four weeks later

"Dex, get in here. You're going to miss the call."

There was a crash and then a string of muttered curses before he appeared; holding what looked like the remnants of a broken vase.

I shook my head. "Another one?"

"I think this is the last one, small saving grace."

"Put it down and come over here. Everyone's waiting."

He placed the jagged shards carefully on a box, which amused me. He's managed to destroy every delicate thing in the apartment, but was now learning to be careful. For someone who could play a bass, and a woman's body with incredible dexterity, when it came to packing up his father's things, he was useless. Some of it was the fact that he hadn't had more than a single glass of wine with dinner since we got to Bristol, but I couldn't help but wonder if there was some other unconscious psychological reason for his recent butter-fingers status.

Before I could think about it too much, the screen on my tablet flashed and then changed. From what I could see the conference room was full. Mostly suits, square guys who'd probably never seen a rock concert. But there, at the end of the table, looking bored was the rest of the band. It was good to see their faces somewhere other than the television and gossip magazines.

"Hullo all," Dex said chirpily. He knew the label was worried, and for some reason decided that talking like he'd become a Stepford bass player was the solution.

"Dex, thanks for taking time to make this call," Ryan said. "We know you are Rebecca are still settling your father's affairs."

That much was true. What they didn't know is we'd just returned to Bristol after spending ten days camping. With no distractions or temptations, it was the perfect place to hide after the funeral. No reporters' questions or festive pubs to lure him.

But no one else needed to know that and we both just nodded.

"Great," Ryan continued. "Now that we're all here, I'll turn this over to Frank."

One of the suits smiled and stood up. I could see Rick sneering behind him.

"Hey gang," the man said lamely. "So glad to get everyone together for a chance to chat. As you know, since I was put in charge of this management team, I've been developing a three year plan to make Dream Defiled not just the talented group of guys you are, but to secure your place in music history. We're firing on all cylinders over here, teams working around the clock."

I struggled to keep from giggling at his long series of clichés, leaning away from the webcam.

WELL ROCKED

"We all know striking while the iron is hot has to be our top priority. Because of that, we're moving some scheduled items around. Instead of sending you all into the studio for the rest of the year, we're moving up the next tour.

"But this won't be the seedy club spots I know you all adore. We're going arena this time. Ten thousand seats. Thirty cities. Then, we'll release a live album and concert film on DVD and streaming to capitalize on the success of the tour. By the time the next album of new material comes out, you boys will be millionaires and Dream Defiled will be a household name.

"Questions, anyone?"

Dex and I just sat there, mouths hanging open. But, ever the front man, Joe managed to form words. "That all sounds great, but are we really ready to headline something like that?"

"Excellent question, Mr. Hawk. The answer is yes. With the plan we've got cooking, every show will sell out."

"How?"

"Easy, we're sending you out with two other amazing acts. The first Playology, I think you've done shows with them before."

Joe nodded. "Yeah, a big festival this spring."

"Great. Their album is doing well too, and you'll rise together."

"Uh-huh. But that still-"

"I wasn't finished. Your tour will also feature the first solo performances of Julia Connor since she was a tiny thing playing state fairs."

Julia Connor. She was some kid television actor slash singer slash dancer or something. I vaguely recalled seeing her mentioned in an email, and had looked her up. She'd spent her teen years, post TV in a girl group that was really

85

popular in Eastern Europe, but hadn't made much of an impact in the States. It seemed like a weird fit for the boys, but I trusted that the label guys knew what they were doing. She was certainly famous enough to fill stadiums. Online I'd been able to track almost every move the girl made from birth. Three years after she'd left the public eye, she still hand hundreds of active fan sites, and a lawsuit pending against some scumbag who stole one of those cherry-pickers the phone company uses, in order to take pictures of her bedroom. If that was the level of fame Dex and the others were headed towards, I wasn't sure it would be a good thing at all.

But then I looked over at him. He was ignoring the meeting and watching me. He grasped my hand and bumped his leg against mine. I relaxed a bit, thinking about all of the wonderful times we'd shared.

Like I'd told him in our darkest hour, we were strong enough to make it through anything. Life, sex, work, death, demons. Fame didn't stand a chance at getting between us.

ABOUT THE AUTHOR

Clara Bayard is a wealthy business owner who, following the brutal death of her parents, used that wealth to create a secret identity and a lot of cool gadgets in order to protect the city she adores, and keep others from experiencing the same pain she did.

Wait, no. That's Batman.

Clara is a just a regular gal living in the Mid-Atlantic region. She loves writing sexy stories about flawed people doing exciting things. When she's not writing she enjoys talking to strangers in bars and marathon-watching TV shows everyone else has seen already.

Connect Online:

www.ClaraBayard.com
Facebook.com/ClaraBayardAuthor
Twitter.com/ClaraBayard

26030600R00056

Made in the USA
Lexington, KY
15 September 2013